DAVID MEETS A FOOTBALL PIONEER

by Linda S

COVER-TO-COVER BOOKS

Perfection Learning®

Cover and Inside
Illustration: Dea Marks

About the Author

Linda Sibley has lived in Harlingen, Texas, her entire life, except for one year away at school. She now lives there with her huband, Rick, and two children, Jeremy and Jennifer.

Ms. Sibley did contract work for attorneys for 15 years so she could be at home to raise her children. Now she is working at a local hospital part-time. This enables her to spend time writing, which is her favorite thing to do. She also enjoys reading and searching for interesting antiques.

Traveling is another of Ms. Sibley's interests. So far she has visited 24 states and 2 countries. She is always looking for an excuse to go on another trip.

For information, contact

Perfection Learning® Corporation

1000 North Second Avenue, P.O. Box 500
Logan, Iowa 51546-0500.
Phone: 1-800-831-4190
Fax: 1-800-543-2745
perfectionlearning.com

Paperback ISBN 0-7891-5677-6
Cover Craft® ISBN 0-7569-0636-9

Contents

1

THE TRIVIA QUESTION

"Touchdown!" I shouted as I jumped up from the floor. I slapped Jeff's hand for a high five. Ryan was busy doing his touchdown dance.

"I knew the Cowboys would catch up!" Dad exclaimed.

It was halftime now. The score was tied at 24. I watched as Dad and my friends whooped and hollered. It reminded me how much I love Sunday afternoons. I always spend them watching football with my best friends.

Dad is always included too. He's been the high school football coach for ten years. We consider him a football expert.

My best friends are Jeff Chandler and Ryan Wilson. We met when our families bought houses on the same block. Ryan's family moved in across the street. Jeff's family bought the house next door. We were only two years old at the time. My little sister, Jenny, wasn't even born yet.

We've always attended the same schools and church. Now we even play on the same football team. During this time of the year, football is almost all we think about.

Our celebration was getting a little too loud. I wasn't surprised to hear Mom yell.

"You guys quiet down!" she shouted from the kitchen. "I'm trying to study in here!"

Hearing her voice made us think about the kitchen. Thinking about the kitchen made us think about food. We decided it was the perfect time to raid the refrigerator.

I jumped on Dad's back as he started for the

kitchen. Ryan seemed to think that was a good idea. He jumped on Jeff's back. When we paraded into the kitchen, Mom didn't look happy.

"We're four hungry men in search of food!" Dad laughed.

"Do you have any chips and dip?" Ryan asked.

"I'd rather have some cookies," Jeff said.

"I just want a big jar of pickles!" I added.

"I'm working on a history test for my class," Mom said. She sounded really annoyed. She had papers spread out all over the kitchen table.

"Sorry, Mom," I said. "We'll be out of your way in a minute."

We grabbed some plates. Quickly, we filled them with our favorite foods.

I laughed as I watched Jeff and Ryan. They were digging through the pantry. They knew exactly where Dad hid his favorite cookies.

We carried our food into the den. We settled in front of our new 52-inch television. Dad had convinced Mom to buy it before football season began. He'd been so excited when it was delivered. He'd been like a kid with a new toy.

"Quiet down," Dad ordered. "I want to hear the trivia question."

"Today's trivia question is a tough one," said the announcer.

"Hah!" Dad smirked. "I know everything about football!"

"This man was the first African American college player," the announcer said. "He broke many records in 1892 and 1893. His honors include being named to the Walter Camp All-America team. He was also chosen team captain at Harvard University."

I looked at Dad. His forehead wrinkled. I'd never known him to miss a trivia question.

"He studied law at Harvard," the announcer went on. "Later he was appointed Assistant U.S. Attorney General by President Taft."

"Can you name this African American pioneer?" asked the announcer. "I'll be back after the commercial to find out."

We looked at Dad and waited. He just sat there, staring off into space.

It was silent except for the crunch of potato chips. When the commercial ended, we looked at Dad again. He still didn't have an answer.

"Now for the answer to today's trivia question," said the announcer. "The young player's name was William Henry Lewis."

"That's amazing," Dad said. "I've never even heard of that guy before."

"That's okay," I tried to reassure him.

"Yeah," Ryan agreed. "I bet no one knew the answer."

Soon we were lost in the second half of the game. The Dallas Cowboys scored a last minute touchdown. We were thrilled when they won 31 to 24.

Dad was quiet during the second half. When the game ended, he disappeared.

After the guys left, I went looking for Dad. I found him in the office. He was sitting at the desk. His glasses were perched on the end of his nose. A stack of books was piled in front of him.

"Hey, Dad!" I said. "What are you doing?"

"I'm looking for information about William Henry Lewis," he said. "He sounds like an interesting guy. I'm having trouble finding anything though."

"Have you forgotten that I'm a computer whiz?" I bragged. "Just let me surf the Internet. I'll find out all about him."

I tried using all my favorite search engines. But I couldn't find much information—just the same things Dad had found. By then, Mom and Jenny had wandered into the office. They decided to join the search too.

We only found a few more details. And that just made us more curious about the mysterious Mr. Lewis.

"I have a good idea," Dad said with a mischievous smile. "There's another way to learn more about him."

Dad paused. We waited to hear his idea.

"We could just ask him," Dad finished and grinned.

"What does that mean?" Jenny asked.

"I think *I* know," Mom said. She eyed Dad carefully. "I think he's proposing a trip in the time machine."

My mom was talking about the time machine my grandpa had built. We found it in the garage after he died. He'd never had a chance to see if it worked. So we decided to test it. We'd been amazed when it actually worked! Since then, we'd taken several trips in Grandpa's great invention.

"You have to admit it would be interesting," Dad said. "We could return to 1893 and meet Mr. Lewis. We've never been to Cambridge, Massachusetts. We could check out Harvard University while we're there."

"Of course, we'd see some football games too," Mom added. She knew Dad well.

"You bet!" Dad said. "Just think how exciting it would be to see an 1893 football game."

He picked up a book from the desk. "I've been looking through this book. It's called *The History of Football*. It tells about the 1893 game of football. It was completely different than our modern game."

"I think the trip is a great idea," I declared.

Playing on the junior high team was just the beginning for me. I planned on playing in high school too. Then I'd get a football scholarship and play for a big university. Afterward, I'd be offered millions of dollars to play in the pros.

"I don't know," Jenny whined. "It doesn't sound like much fun to me. I get tired of hearing about football all the time."

"The whole trip wouldn't be about football," Dad said. "We could do some sightseeing in Massachusetts. We might even see some snow."

"Snow?" Jenny asked. I could see that she was a little more interested now.

"He's right," Mom agreed. "Just imagine the crisp, cold air. It would be a nice break from these warm October days in Texas."

Jenny was silent. I wasn't sure what she was thinking. That always made me nervous.

"Does everyone agree?" asked Dad hopefully. "Shall we plan a trip to Massachusetts in 1893?"

"It's okay with me," Mom offered.

"You can count me in," I said enthusiastically. "I definitely want to go."

"Jenny?" Dad asked. "What do you think?"

"O—kay," she agreed slowly. "But I still think it sounds kind of boring." She slumped down in her chair unhappily. Little did she know how much she would enjoy meeting William Henry Lewis.

2

THE HANDSOME STRANGER

"We're definitely going to Massachusetts," Dad said the next day. "It's going to be a short trip though. We'll leave this Friday and return the following Tuesday."

"Why are we going for such a short time?" I asked.

"Your mother and I don't like for you to miss school," Dad said. "There's no school on Monday because it's Columbus Day. You'll still miss one day on Tuesday. We don't want you to miss any more than that."

"We'll call your schools tomorrow," Mom said. "We'll explain that we're going out of town. We'll get any work that you're going to miss."

"Four days isn't going to be enough time," I complained.

"It will be long enough," Dad tried to assure me. "We'll arrive in Cambridge on a Friday evening. It will be November 24, 1893. Then we'll return at midnight the following Tuesday."

"Midnight?" Jenny asked. "Why are we coming home at midnight?"

"We decided it's safer to leave during the night," Mom said. "That way no one will ask questions about how we're traveling."

"That's true," I agreed. "But will we be able to see a football game?"

"Yes, sir!" Dad grinned. "There's going to be a game on Saturday. Harvard will play their rival, Yale University."

"Then we'll still have three more days," Mom added. "Hopefully, we can find a way to meet Mr. Lewis."

"Sounds like a good plan to me," I said happily.

"At least it will be a short trip," Jenny muttered.

Mom ignored Jenny's remark. "Be prepared to leave on Friday," Mom said.

"David, we'll need to do a few things before we leave," Dad said. "We'll need to mow the—"

I was lucky the phone rang before he could finish. Hopefully, he'd forget about mowing the lawn.

"I'll get it," I said quickly. I rushed out of the room to answer the phone. The call was from Jeff.

"That new movie starts on Saturday," he said excitedly. "Ryan says he can go. We can meet at my house. Then we'll go to the 7:00 show."

"That sounds great!" I said. Then I remembered our trip.

"Oh, I forgot," I mumbled. "My family is going out of town this weekend."

"Where are you going?" he asked.

"Well—uh—I'm not sure yet," I stammered. "I mean—my parents want to go somewhere. They just haven't decided where."

"Do you have to go too?" he asked. "You could spend the weekend at my house. Jeff could come over too."

"No, I'm sorry," I said. "I have to go with them. I'll have to see the movie when I get back."

"Well, okay," he said, sounding disappointed.

When I hung up the phone, I felt guilty. I really hated lying to my friends. It was a problem whenever we traveled in the time machine. Each time, it got harder to come up with excuses.

Jeff and Ryan would be shocked if they knew the truth. I *wanted* to tell them. Instead, I had to be careful not to let anything slip.

———————◆———————

Our week passed quickly. Jenny and I made up the schoolwork we would miss. Dad made sure we got the yard mowed too.

Mom spent some time in the local antique shops. Shopping for old clothes had become her favorite pastime. She'd gradually built up a sizable wardrobe for us.

We picked out some warm clothes to wear. Mom packed them into our old, worn suitcase.

We went to Grandma's right after school on Friday. She was in the garage getting the time machine ready. She'd polished the metal capsule and windows. She was admiring Grandpa's invention when we arrived.

"Are you sure you don't want to go along?" I asked her.

"No, I'm going to skip this one," she said. "But I'll be anxious to hear all about it when you get back."

We said our good-byes and filed into the time machine.

DAVID MEETS A FOOTBALL PIONEER

I was the last one into the capsule. I shut the heavy metal door behind me. Dad set the controls and started our ride through time.

Immediately, bright lights began to swirl around us. I felt as if I were spinning in circles. I could hear distant voices that slowly grew softer. In only a few seconds, we were transported to 1893.

When the ride stopped, we were standing in a pasture. Scattered patches of snow lay on the ground. Towering elm trees surrounded the field. It was kind of cool—very quiet and peaceful.

We looked around and saw buildings in the distance. We knew it must be Cambridge, so we headed that direction.

While we walked, I got a look at the countryside. Several inches of snow lined the sides of the dirt road.

Millions of dry leaves covered the ground. I marched right through the deepest piles. I'd always hated raking leaves at home. But I had fun jumping in the big piles. I'd end up scattering the leaves everywhere and then have to rake them again.

The soft winds were chilly. I had to pull the collar up on my wool coat. It was hard to believe I'd been wearing shorts that morning.

As we walked into town, it felt so weird. It was as if we'd walked into an old Western movie. I wouldn't have been surprised if Clint Eastwood had walked out of the livery stable.

We stopped at the only hotel in town. It wasn't anything like our modern hotels. I didn't bother to look for a swimming pool or hot tub. We didn't complain though. We were pleased they would rent us a room.

Dad carried our suitcase upstairs. We decided to wait outside on the wooden porch. We were anxious to look around Cambridge before dark.

First we went to Harvard. It was founded in 1636. That made it the oldest university in America. We strolled around the quaint little campus. Young men were gathered in groups on the lawn.

"Where are all the girls?" Jenny asked.

"Only men attended Harvard in 1893," Mom said.

"What?" she exclaimed. "No girls? That's ridiculous."

I had to agree that it didn't seem fair.

"I wonder what's going on tonight," I said. "All the guys are dressed up."

"They dress like that all the time," Mom said.

"You're kidding!" I said in disbelief.

"The young men are expected to dress up," Dad agreed. "They wear a suit and tie every day to class."

"I'm sure glad times have changed," I said.

I hadn't worn a suit and tie since Aunt Sally's wedding. I'd been miserable. The coat was too hot, and the tie almost choked me to death.

"Ouch!" Jenny cried loudly.

I spun around to find her sprawled out on the grass. She must have tripped over something.

A young black man was helping her to her feet. His back was toward us, so we couldn't see his face. We watched as he dusted her off. Then he tipped his hat in greeting.

"You're a mighty pretty little lady," he said.

"Th—thank you," she said, smiling.

"Can I help you with something?" he asked.

"N—no," she stuttered.

I'd never heard Jenny stutter before. That fall must have done some real damage.

"Hello," Dad interrupted. "Thanks for helping my daughter."

The young man turned around to face us.

"You're very welcome," he said kindly.

"My name is Tom Smithers," Dad said.

The handsome young man smiled and stuck out his hand.

"It's a pleasure to meet you, Mr. Smithers," he said politely. "My name is William Henry Lewis."

An Unusual Football Game

"*You're* William Henry Lewis?" I asked, astonished.

He looked at me in surprise.

"You're the reason we came to Cambridge," Dad explained. "We want to see you play football tomorrow against Yale."

"That's very kind," William said, grinning. "I guess I'll see you in Springfield."

I looked at Dad and saw his smile fade away.

"Springfield?" he gulped.

"Yes, sir," William said. "The game is in Springfield. In fact, I think the last train already left. Have you made other plans to get there?"

"Tom!" Mom said as she gave him a stern look. I knew that look. Usually it was directed at me.

"I just assumed the game would be in Cambridge," Dad said pitifully.

"Don't worry, Mr. Smithers," William said. "I'll make sure you and your family get there."

"How are you going to do that?" Mom asked.

"The football team travels on its own train," he explained. "I'll get permission for you to ride with the team."

"You could do that?" I asked in amazement.

I was thrilled! Everything was working out perfectly. We'd already met William. And now I'd get to ride with the Harvard football team.

"That would be great to ride with the players!" Dad said.

"Just meet me at the station at 5:30 a.m.," William instructed.

"We'll be there!" Dad and I said together.

William bowed again to Jenny and tipped his hat.

She smiled that same googly-eyed smile. That's when I figured it out. She had a crush on William! She didn't seem to care that he was 16 years older than she was.

After our chance meeting, we returned to the hotel. We were talking excitedly as we climbed the stairs to the second floor.

"Hold on a second," I said to the others. "I want to check something out."

I'd noticed a door at the end of the hall. It had a sign that read *PRIVY*. I opened the door and took a quick look around.

"Well, it doesn't have a Jacuzzi," I laughed. "But it's still better than an outhouse."

Everyone agreed that anything would be better than an outhouse.

Our hotel room was barely furnished. A frayed rug decorated the wooden floor. A stand with a pitcher of water and two hard back chairs stood in the corner.

Unfortunately, there was only one small bed. So Dad and I offered to sleep on the floor. We didn't care if it was uncomfortable. We were too excited about going to the game.

We were awake bright and early the next morning. The sky was clear, and the air was cold. It looked like perfect weather for a football game.

We ate a quick breakfast. Afterward, Jenny insisted on going back upstairs. She said she'd only be a few minutes. But she took a lot longer than a few minutes. We were almost late to meet William.

"I was afraid you'd miss the train," William said.

"We were waiting for Jenny," I groaned. "She had to fix her hair."

Jenny looked as if she wanted to punch me.

"Well, it was worth the wait." William smiled at her. "You look lovely, Miss Jenny."

She grinned at William. When he turned away, she stuck out her tongue at me.

We boarded the train with the Harvard team. William introduced us to Coach Stewart. I couldn't believe I got to shake the coach's hand.

William also introduced us to all of his teammates. I was surprised that they weren't big and muscular. They had wiry, slender bodies. They looked tough though. It was easy to see they were in perfect physical condition.

They were dressed in turtleneck sweaters with a big H on front. They wore knickers with tall, thick stockings and soft boots.

"Wait until you see our new uniforms," William said proudly. "They're made of leather instead of canvas and moleskin. They were made by a tailor and cost $125.00 each."

Even *I* knew how impressive that was. Our trips were teaching me the value of money during different time periods. That was a lot of money for one uniform in 1893.

I was captivated by their stories of past games. The players were eager to brag about their victories. They even reenacted one of their winning plays on the train.

One of the players passed the ball to William. He ran down the center aisle but was tackled by his teammate. The two of them laughed as they slid down the aisle. They were still laughing when they bumped their heads on the door.

We arrived in Springfield to a waiting crowd. Hundreds of people gathered along the train tracks. The crowds applauded and cheered as the players left the train. They were still cheering as the players boarded their carriages.

It was fun to be a part of the excitement. All around us, fans were waving hundreds of crimson banners. I joined in and chanted, "Hurray for Harvard."

Dad told William we would walk to Hampden Park. William asked if I could stay with him.

"Me?" I asked in surprise.

"I want you to see the game up close." He smiled.

I followed him into a waiting carriage. The guys were excited and laughing as we rode to the park. They teased me about being their replacement player.

When we arrived, we were ushered into a big room. There were no lockers. The players just threw their clothes everywhere in the rush to change.

As the players filed out of the building, I got a look at Hampden Park. I had no idea so many people would be there. Someone said about 25,000 people had come to watch. College football was more popular in 1893 than I'd realized.

The Yale Bulldogs began filing onto the field. When they appeared, their fans cheered loudly.

Their uniforms were similar to Harvard's. They wore shirts covered by sleeveless canvas jackets. The jackets were laced tightly up the front. They also wore knickers with heavy blue stockings.

It surprised me that neither team wore protective equipment. They didn't have padding on their thighs or hips. They also didn't have on shoulder pads. But I was really surprised that they didn't even wear helmets!

I watched from the sidelines as the Harvard Crimsons filed onto the field. The fans cheered once again and waved their crimson flags. I'd expected a quiet little football game. But it was far from quiet!

I stayed right on the sidelines. It was wild to be so close to the players. I couldn't take my eyes off the game. It was played differently than any football game I'd ever seen.

Like William, I played center position on my team. I would hike the ball back to the quarterback. Then the quarterback would pass the ball or hand it off to another player.

William actually rolled the ball back with his feet to the quarterback. It was like a combination of rugby and football.

Another big difference was the formations. When I played football, we played one-against-one. In this game, a big group of players could stay together.

First the ball was put into play. Then the group charged toward the other team. They just mowed them down! That would clear a path for the player carrying the football.

Yale was the first to score. Their fullback, Frank Butterworth, made the run. It was followed with a kick by Bill Hickok. That brought the score to 6 to 0 in favor of Yale.

During halftime, Coach Stewart gave the team a pep talk. They were all worked up when they returned to play. I was sure they'd win.

The Yale students were still putting on their halftime show. Over 1,000 students sat together in the grandstands. They sang several fight songs.

Hurray! Hurray then for the blue!

Hurray! Hurray! Hurray for Captain Hinkey too!

We'll triumph over Harvard in the way we always do!

Down with the Crimson forever!

The second half of the game was just as exciting.

The crowds never stopped cheering. And neither did I. I even saw Jenny stand up and cheer for Harvard.

Unfortunately, the captain of Harvard's team was injured. He had to be carried off the field. Another Harvard player went out on the field to replace him.

William played the entire game. His only break was during halftime. I hadn't realized the players had to play the entire game. Football players in 1893 had to be tough!

Harvard never recovered after losing its captain. The game ended with a score of Yale 6, Harvard 0.

The team was disappointed about the loss. But they were already talking about the next game. They were confident they'd win their game against Pennsylvania.

I'd always thought of myself as a big Dallas Cowboys fan. But the Harvard team had really earned my respect. I was going to be their new number one fan!

4

LIFE IN CAMBRIDGE

On the ride back to Cambridge, the mood on the train had changed. Everyone was much quieter. I knew they must be exhausted.

"What did you think of the game?" William asked Dad.

"It was pretty amazing," Dad said.

"Will you be here for the game on Thanksgiving?" William asked.

"Unfortunately, we have to leave Tuesday evening," Dad said. "It's too bad though. We'd love to see you play again."

"Are you staying in Cambridge through Tuesday?" William asked.

"Yeah, we're staying in the hotel there," I answered.

"I'd be happy to show you around town," William said politely. Then he looked at Jenny and grinned. "Would that be all right with you, Miss Jenny?"

"That would be great," Jenny said, smiling brightly.

"But tomorrow is Sunday," Dad reminded us. "We need to go to church."

"You're welcome to join me," William offered. "I can meet you in front of the hotel. We can all walk together."

Dad thanked William for the invitation. We were thrilled to have a tour guide.

When we arrived in Cambridge, it was late. We made final plans to meet William the next morning. Then we went straight to bed.

The next morning, the temperature was warmer. The sky was clear. It was a great day to be outside.

William was at the hotel promptly at 8:30. He

looked handsome in his dark suit. He offered Jenny his arm. She held her head high as they strolled ahead of us.

We'd seen a large white church building when we arrived. It had a tall steeple with a big church bell inside. But William took us to a different church—the church for blacks.

It was smaller than the one we'd seen. It had a short steeple above the front door. And there was no church bell.

The small building was packed with people. The preacher barely had room to stand in front.

An old organ was pressed against the wall. It was played by a young, pretty organist. She was able to make that old organ play beautiful music.

The church didn't have fancy pews, carpeting, and central heating like ours. But everyone was happy and friendly. We really enjoyed the service.

Afterward, we stood outside with William. He introduced us to all of his friends. Suddenly the organist appeared at his side.

When he turned and saw her, he smiled widely. He reached over and kissed her on the cheek. Jenny stared at them in surprise.

"I'd like to introduce this beautiful lady," William said proudly. "This is my wife, Elizabeth."

"My goodness!" Mom said in surprise. "Where

have you been hiding this young lady?"

"I wasn't feeling well yesterday," Elizabeth explained. "That's why I missed the game."

"This morning she went to the church early to practice," William explained. "She also made us a picnic lunch. It will be quite a treat. She's the best cook in Cambridge."

Elizabeth smiled at his compliment. She reached over to take his hand. Then she turned and looked at Jenny.

"You must be Jenny," she said in a soft voice. "I've heard all about you. It's a pleasure to finally meet you."

"Thanks," Jenny mumbled as she stared at the ground.

It was obvious that she wasn't happy. She hadn't realized William had another girl in his life. Jenny stayed behind us as we walked. She kept her head down and kicked stones that lay on the ground.

It was an unusually warm day for November. We decided to have a real picnic outside.

William led us down to the Charles River. We set up our picnic near a gristmill. I'd never even heard of a gristmill before. Dad explained it was used to grind grain into flour.

We spread a blanket under a big elm tree. Then we covered the blanket with our feast. Elizabeth had baked ham, sweet potatoes, and fresh bread. My favorite was the lemon pie.

William said everybody loved Elizabeth's pies. She even sold them in town.

Elizabeth brought her jelly and jam for us to sample too. She made them from cranberries that grew wild in that area.

We stayed all afternoon and talked. William brought along his football. He taught me some of the drills his team performed.

While we were tossing around the football, William told stories of life at Harvard. Most were interesting or funny. But some of his stories made me mad. Cambridge wasn't always friendly to people like William.

Once, he'd gone to get a haircut at a local barbershop. It was the same barbershop where most Harvard students went. But the owner had refused to give him a haircut. He said he wouldn't cut a black man's hair. It made William angry just to repeat the story.

He swore he was going to speak to a state legislator. He wanted new laws passed that would prevent discrimination. He hoped his law degree would help him make changes someday.

I thought about what William said as we packed up our picnic. Fighting discrimination was going to be difficult. He'd have some tough battles ahead of him.

When we reached the hotel, William asked us about our plans for the next day.

"We appreciate your kindness," Dad said. "But aren't we keeping you from your classes or work?"

"I can meet you after my morning class," William said. "Then I'll give you a tour of Harvard. When we finish, I'll go to work at the law office. My job as a clerk only requires a few hours each day."

I wanted to spend more time with William. And a tour of Harvard sounded like a great idea. We made plans to meet William the next morning.

It was already dark when we climbed the stairs to our hotel room. Without electricity, we couldn't do much after dark. I would have liked to watch TV for a while. But the bare little room offered nothing but a place to sleep.

———◆———

The next morning, we were early. We were anxious to start our tour. Finally, William's class let out.

The first stop on campus was Memorial Hall. It was a memorial for graduates who fought for the Union in the Civil War. The brick building was huge. It had a tower that soared 195 feet tall.

"There's a story that goes with that tower," William said. "Every fall, a brave player climbs the tower. He carries with him a crimson flag. When he reaches the top, he places it on the top pinnacle."

"That sounds dangerous," Mom commented.

"Yes, it is," agreed William as we walked inside. "But someone succeeds in posting the flag each year."

The stained glass windows in the hall were amazing. Each window had a story behind it. William explained how one window was known as the Battle Window. It was made in 1860. The window honored 12 classmates who had died in the Civil War.

Sanders Theater was also a part of Memorial Hall. Harvard students held their graduation ceremonies there. I imagined myself walking across the stage and accepting my college diploma someday.

I was surprised when I saw the dining hall. The tables were set in long rows. They were covered with white tablecloths and nice dishes. It looked like a fancy restaurant. It sure didn't look like my school cafeteria.

The next stop on the tour was Austin Hall. That was where William's law classes were held. We walked down the long hallway. The heavily polished wooden floors and walls were spotless. Some of the classroom doors were open. We could see the classes in progress as we passed by.

As I walked, I studied the paintings on the walls. They were portraits of former Harvard students who became presidents. Pictures of John Adams and John Quincy Adams hung there. An image of Rutherford B. Hayes stared at me.

The opposite wall was blank. I studied it thoughtfully. I imagined paintings of future Harvard students who would become presidents. Those included Theodore Roosevelt, Franklin D. Roosevelt, and John F. Kennedy.

I was standing in the place where six presidents would attend college. Just thinking about it gave me goose bumps.

I stared at the blank place on the wall again. What if I were elected president someday? After all, it was possible. I tried to imagine *my* picture hanging there. Then I really got goose bumps!

5

OLD-FASHIONED ENTERTAINMENT

Elizabeth joined us for a late lunch. I was happy to see she'd brought another picnic basket. This time, the cold air forced us inside. When we finished eating, the basket was completely empty.

Elizabeth suggested we take a walk down Main Street. In front of the hotel, I saw a boy riding an unusual bicycle. It had handlebars and pedals like normal bikes. But the front tire was over four feet tall. And the rear tire was only about 15 inches tall.

"Hey, Dad!" I yelled. I grabbed his arm to get his attention. "Look at that bike."

"Haven't you seen a bicycle like that before?" William asked.

"No," I said in surprise. "I've never seen anything like it."

William whistled at the boy. He rode in our direction. He looked so funny perched over that big wheel. I watched in amazement as he pedaled toward us. He stopped the bike next to a building so he could jump off.

"Hi, Casey," William greeted. "Would you mind if my friend tried your bicycle?"

"Naw," he grinned. "Go ahead and give it a try."

I couldn't even get on the bicycle without help. Dad had to hoist me up to the seat.

It looked great with its leather seat and nickel-plated handlebars. But it sure was difficult to ride. I felt as if I were riding a bicycle on stilts.

"Too bad you don't have the video camera," I called to Dad. Instantly, I realized what I'd said.

I looked back to see if William had heard me. That

wasn't a smart thing to do. I ran right into the porch of the hotel. The jolt sent me flying over the handlebars. It was quite a drop from those handlebars! Luckily, I only got a couple of scrapes. I decided I would stick to my own bike.

William had to go to work after that. Elizabeth invited us back to their house. Jenny was thrilled. She'd gotten over her jealously and had come to like Elizabeth.

William and Elizabeth lived in a modest little house near Harvard. They didn't have any luxuries, but their home was very comfortable.

"I have something you might like, Jenny," Elizabeth said. "Professor Chambers loaned them to William. They're called stereoscopes."

"What do you do with them?" Jenny asked.

"You look at pictures," Elizabeth explained.

The odd glasses looked similar to a pair of binoculars. Elizabeth took them and placed a picture card inside. She held them to Jenny's face.

"Wow!" Jenny said. "These are terrific!"

"Let me see," I said.

The picture card had two identical pictures side by side. When you looked through the stereoscope, the pictures blended into one. Then they looked three-dimensional. It made you feel as if you were inside the picture. It reminded me of a 3-D movie I'd seen once.

Jenny and I took turns going through the picture cards. A view of a steam train in Switzerland appeared. There was also a great photo of a clipper ship. It was caught in the ice in Boston Harbor.

"Have you ever played a card game?" Elizabeth asked.

"We play cards all the time," Jenny said.

"I have this totem card game," she offered.

I'd never thought about people playing card games in 1893.

Elizabeth handed Jenny a small tin can full of cards. It didn't look like any card game we'd ever played. But we decided to give it a try.

The deck had 37 cards. They had pictures of birds and animals on them. You learned facts about them as you played. The object of the game was to get the totem card.

We played for a while until we got bored. I asked Mom and Dad if we could go outside. It wasn't quite dark yet. I figured we'd have plenty of light to explore more of Cambridge.

"It's awfully cold," Mom warned.

I assured her we'd stay warm. Finally she agreed. Jenny pulled on her coat and followed me.

"What are we going to do?" she asked.

"Just follow me," I directed her. "I want to go look at Memorial Hall again."

"It's cold and almost dark," she complained. "You're not going to be able to see anything."

Out of curiosity, she followed me anyway. When we got to Memorial Hall, I studied the tower.

"I bet I could climb that tower," I said.

"David!" she fumed. "You're not going to try climbing that tower, are you?"

"Other guys have done it," I reasoned. "It can't be that hard."

"It doesn't look like there's anything to hold on to," she warned.

"Look!" I said, totally ignoring her. "I could start there on the corner. I could catch hold of that window casing. It would be an easy climb to the second floor. Then I'd be at the base of the tower."

"You're crazy, David Smithers!" she fussed. "You're going to kill yourself."

"Girls!" I said under my breath. "What do they know anyway?"

I reached around to feel my back pocket. A crimson flag was tucked there. This would be a cinch.

I went around to the corner of the building and hoisted myself up. Jenny stood underneath me, fussing all the while.

I made it to the second level easily. I crawled over to the base of the tower. From there I could see it would be more difficult than I'd realized.

I reached around on the side of the tower. I felt around for something to hold on to. Small wooden pegs jutted out of the brick. They were only a couple of inches long, but I figured they'd work.

I grabbed hold of one and lifted myself about 12 inches. Then I felt on the other side. I found another one and lifted myself again. I ran my foot along the tower until I found a foothold.

I began to slowly work my way up the tower. My entire body was balanced on two-inch pegs!

I could hear Jenny calling for me to be careful. But I felt confident and continued to make the long climb. At last I could see the top of the tower just above me.

I felt for another peg but couldn't find it. So I stretched up as far as I could reach. My fingertips just reached the top level. Very slowly, I pulled myself up to the top of the tower.

I'd made it! Triumphantly, I placed the crimson flag on the pinnacle. I watched for a minute as the flag waved in the soft nighttime breeze.

I felt totally unstoppable. I'd accomplished something that most college students feared doing. I couldn't wait to tell William. He'd be so impressed.

"Get down, David!" Jenny called. "And be careful."

"Okay, okay," I said. "I'm starting down now."

The truth was that I was freezing now. I was pretty

anxious to get down myself.

I carefully lowered myself over the edge of the tower. I slid my foot down the wall in search of a peg.

I couldn't find one, so I tried the other foot. No luck. I didn't dare look down. I needed to stay firmly pressed against the cold brick. If I leaned away from the tower, I'd fall for sure.

I was beginning to get a little concerned. But I wasn't ready to panic yet. I was sure I'd think of something.

Finally, I felt a peg under my left foot. I took a deep breath and tried to relax. Then I began to work my way down slowly, one peg at a time.

Without warning, I felt the peg under my right foot give way. I listened as it fell against the roof of the building. Panic crept over me when I realized I'd lost my foothold. Then I lost my balance and began sliding down the tower.

I strained to dig my fingernails into the cold brick. At last I was able to stop myself. I clung to the tower as tightly as I could. I knew that the slightest movement would send me crashing down almost 193 feet!

6

A Disastrous Accident

"David!" Jenny screamed. "Are you all right?"

My face was pressed hard against the tower. I could barely talk.

"Get help," I said as loudly as I could. I knew she heard me. I could hear her footsteps as she took off running.

I struggled to hang on. My fingertips ached from the cold. I knew they must be bleeding from the roughness of the brick.

My muscles were tired. I wanted to shift positions. But there was no way that I could move. Even my breathing could shake me from my hold.

It seemed like an eternity before Jenny returned with everyone.

"Hold on, David!" Dad called. "I'm coming to get you!"

"No," I heard William insist. "I'll go."

I was so glad to hear his voice. I was afraid he'd still be at work.

"Be careful, William," Elizabeth called.

I could hear him making his way onto the roof.

"Hold on tight, David!" William said. "I'll be there in just a minute."

I hung on as tightly as I could. I was scared to death that I would fall. I was also very embarrassed at being stuck on the tower. At least there wasn't anyone else around to see me.

William grabbed hold of the pegs and worked his way up. Finally he was beside me. He put his arm around my waist.

"Slide your left foot down," he instructed. "There's a peg four inches below it."

I did just as he instructed.

"Now slide your right foot down about six inches," he said.

At last I was balanced on the pegs. I took a deep breath and tried to relax.

We began to slowly work our way down the tower. William talked quietly as we worked. It helped keep me calm.

We continued down until the rooftop looked close. Then I decided I'd just jump the rest of the way. I took my foot off one of the pegs so I could jump.

Immediately, I saw that was a bad idea. The roof was farther away than I'd realized. I panicked and grabbed for William. That caused William to completely lose his balance.

We struggled to steady ourselves again. But we'd both lost our grip on the tower. I finally just let go and jumped to the roof. It was an 8-foot drop, but I landed on my feet.

William was never able to recover his balance. He fell nearby and hit the roof with a thud. I saw him wince in pain. He'd fallen on a jagged edge of the roof. Even in the dim light, I saw blood on his leg.

Dad heard us hit and was on the roof in seconds. Together, we helped William to the ground.

Even in the darkness, we could see blood pouring from William's leg. Dad pulled off his belt and wrapped it around the leg above the wound. He said it would work as a tourniquet to slow the bleeding. Then Elizabeth wrapped her wool scarf over the wound.

William leaned on Dad and Elizabeth as he hobbled home. Once inside, Elizabeth placed the kerosene lantern close to him. She unwrapped the bloody scarf. Then she pulled back his torn, bloody trousers to examine his leg. A nasty gash about six inches long ran down his left thigh.

"We need to get a doctor," Mom said.

"No!" exclaimed William. "I don't want anyone to find out. They'll kick me off the football team for sure."

"But you need medical care," Dad tried to reason.

"We have a good friend named Thomas," Elizabeth said. "He's studying medicine. We can send for him. He'll come and look at William's leg. Maybe he can help."

She gave directions to Dad. He rushed out of the house to find Thomas.

Meanwhile, I sat quietly near the fireplace. I didn't even care that my fingers were scraped and bloody. I was so ashamed. My moment of triumph had ended in disaster. It was all my fault that William had gotten hurt.

Dad returned quickly with Thomas. He took one look at the leg and went to work. First he cleaned the wound. Then he sewed the gash together as best he could.

There was no pain medicine to give William. He cried out in pain as Thomas worked.

Thomas carefully wrapped William's leg with clean bandages. He thought the bleeding was under control. There was nothing else he could do. He promised he'd check on William the next day.

We stayed awake all night watching over William. He slept fitfully through the night. Sometimes he would moan loudly in his sleep.

Jenny sat in a chair next to him. She kept a cool cloth on his forehead. She refused to leave his side all night.

The next day, William seemed weaker. Elizabeth cooked his favorite soup. But he was only able to eat a few bites.

We stayed inside all day with him. We didn't know what to do.

After lunch, I heard Mom whispering to Dad. She said William felt as if he had a fever.

Thomas arrived late in the afternoon. He confirmed that William did have a fever. He said the wound was probably infected.

"What does that mean?" Elizabeth asked with tears

in her eyes.

"It means he could lose his leg," Thomas said quietly.

William heard what he said and started to cry out.

"Elizabeth!" he cried. "You can't let them amputate my leg!"

"William," she said, trying to calm him. "You're going to be all right. I'm going to take care of you."

"If he's not better by morning," Thomas said softly, "you need to find Doc Jensen. He'll decide if he needs to amputate."

As soon as Thomas left, Elizabeth put on her coat.

"I have to go to Granny's," Elizabeth said to Mom. "She knows how to mix cures. She'll make me something to put on his leg. That's our only chance."

"Okay," Mom said, looking doubtful. "We'll stay here with William."

After Elizabeth left, Mom was whispering to Dad again.

"You know that's not going to help," she said.

"I know," he said, hanging his head. "But what are we going to do?"

"How did this happen?" Mom said in frustration.

"I know how it happened," I moaned. "It's my fault. It's all my fault."

"It was just an accident, son." Dad tried to comfort me.

"I shouldn't have climbed that stupid tower!" I shouted. "Then none of this would have happened."

Nothing they said would console me. I was devastated at what I'd done. Losing a leg would be horrible for anyone. But for an athlete, it was even more tragic.

William's fever climbed that evening. He slept most of the time. We tried to wake him occasionally and give him food and water. Elizabeth had placed her granny's poultice on his leg. So far there hadn't been any change.

Mom and Dad walked outside. I followed them.

"We're set to go back at midnight tonight," Mom said with tears in her eyes. "But how can we leave William now?"

"I don't know what to do," Dad said in frustration.

"I know what to do," I suggested timidly.

They both turned and looked at me.

"We can take him back home with us," I said.

They opened their mouths to speak but then stopped.

"We can get him the medicine he needs," I continued. "When he gets well, we can bring him back."

Mom and Dad looked at each other.

"Do you think it would work, Tom?" Mom asked.

"It would be awfully risky," Dad said, shaking his

head. "I can think of a hundred reasons why we shouldn't try it."

"But, Dad," I pleaded, "he'll lose his leg. And he might even die."

"I guess you're right," he said with a worried voice. "We really don't have any choice. We'll have to take William home with us."

7

A DESPERATE PLAN

"This is frustrating!" Elizabeth cried. "I have to do something to help. I think I'll go back and talk to Granny. Maybe there's something else she can do."

Because Elizabeth was upset, Jenny volunteered to go along. The rest of us put the plan into motion.

We were able to waken William, but he was still groggy. We explained how we really lived in the future. We told him we could get the medical help he needed.

As we talked, he stared at us with glassy eyes. We weren't sure that he understood us. But he answered "yes" when we asked if we could take him to the future.

When Elizabeth returned, she was in tears. Jenny was close to tears too.

"There's nothing else Granny can do," Elizabeth said sadly.

"You're so exhausted," Mom said gently. "I'm going to fix you some warm milk. You need to get some sleep."

"No," Elizabeth protested. "I need to stay awake. William might need me."

"I promise I'll take care of him," Mom told her. "Please lie down and get some rest."

After more convincing, Elizabeth agreed to try to rest. Only a few minutes passed before she was sleeping soundly.

Quickly, we filled Jenny in on the plan. Then Dad and I hitched the horses to the carriage and brought it to the front door. It took all four of us to carry William to the carriage. He'd fallen into a deep sleep. He didn't even know what was going on.

We carefully placed William in the carriage. Then we covered him with a thick layer of blankets.

Dad drove the carriage to the pasture. He tied the horses' reins securely to a fence post. We struggled in the darkness to carry William.

We made it to the correct place on time. We waited just a couple of minutes. Then the time machine transported us home.

When the ride stopped, Grandma was waiting. She smiled and opened the door of the time capsule. Then she gasped when she saw William lying on the floor.

"Who is that?" she asked in shock. "And what's wrong with him?"

"We'll explain later," Mom said hurriedly. "Right now we need to get him to the hospital."

"David," Dad instructed, "call Ryan's house. His dad will know what to do. Tell him it's an emergency."

Dad and Mom loaded the unconscious William into the van. Mom handed me the cell phone as we tore out of the driveway. I made the call. Ryan answered.

"I don't have time to talk," I told Ryan quickly. "My dad needs to talk to your dad. It's an emergency!"

I handed the phone to Dad.

"Bill, we have an emergency here," Dad tried to explain. "Can you meet us at the hospital?"

"He'll meet us there," Dad said, hanging up the phone.

Luckily, we'd left our clothes in the back of the van. Mom, Jenny, and I changed on the way. When we got to the hospital, Dad switched clothes quickly.

We helped place William on a stretcher. Then Mom and Dad followed the stretcher into the examining room. Jenny and I had to stay in the waiting area.

I sank down into one of the chairs. That's when I realized how exhausted I was. I hadn't slept since the accident. I felt so guilty. I wondered if I'd ever be able to sleep again.

What if William lost his leg? Or what if he died? How could I ever live with myself?

Jenny turned and looked at me. It was as if she were reading my mind.

"He'll be all right," she said softly. "He has to be all right."

I turned away and looked out the window. I didn't want her to see my tears.

It seemed like forever before Mom returned.

"Dr. Wilson has cleaned and sewn up the cut," Mom explained. "They put antibiotic solution on the wound. They're also giving him antibiotics through a tube in his arm."

"Is he going to be okay?" I asked, swallowing hard. I wasn't sure if I wanted to hear the answer.

"We don't know yet," Mom said quietly. "We won't know for at least another 24 hours."

"I'm going to take you to Grandma's house," she declared. "You need to clean up and get some rest."

"No, Mom," I pleaded. "I have to stay here."

"Me too," Jenny said. "I want to see William."

"There's nothing either of you can do," she

insisted. "You both need some rest. You have school tomorrow."

"Mom!" I exclaimed. "There's no way I can go to school."

"I'm sorry, David," she said. "I understand that you're worried about William. But both of you have to go to school."

I started to argue again, but she held up her hands.

"Stop!" she demanded. "William is in good hands. We'll make sure he's taken care of. When school is out tomorrow, you can come to the hospital."

We finally gave in and followed her to the van. When we arrived at Grandma's, she wanted us to eat. But I couldn't. I just wanted to sleep and forget everything.

The next morning, my first thought was of William. I dashed into Grandma's kitchen to find out any news.

"I talked to your mother earlier," she said. "There's no change in William's condition."

We ate our breakfast in silence. Grandma gave us a ride to school. I went straight to class. I wanted to avoid seeing my friends.

Jeff and Ryan finally found me at lunch. They started firing questions at me. I told them I didn't feel very well. I promised I'd tell them all about it later.

Mom was waiting for me when I got out of school. She drove me straight to the hospital. On the way, she explained that William was still unconscious.

When we entered William's room, he looked as if he were sleeping peacefully. He had a tube going into his arm. A monitor kept track of his heart rate. A blood pressure machine was automatically checking his pressure every few minutes. His leg was heavily bandaged.

I pulled a chair close to his bed and sat down. I was determined to keep watch until he opened his eyes.

Mom came in and out of the room. She made phone calls for her and Dad. They were trying to rearrange their schedules. Everything seemed like such a mess.

Late in the afternoon, Dad called to check on William. Mom took her cell phone and walked into the hall.

Shortly after she left, I saw William's hand move. I quickly jumped up and stood over him. He was stirring around very lightly.

"William," I said softly. "Can you hear me?"

His eyes slowly opened. He began to scan the room. At first he looked confused. Gradually, the look on his face changed to panic.

"Where am I?" he called out. "What's happened to me?"

I tried to calm him down. But he kept trying to sit up. Mom had heard him cry out. She came running into the room.

"It's all right, William," she said calmly. "It's me, Annie Smithers. And David is right here too."

"Where am I?" William repeated. "What kind of place is this?"

"It's a hospital," she tried to explain. "Do you remember you had an accident?"

He looked at his bandaged leg and nodded.

"Do you remember what we told you?" she asked. "We told you we would take you home with us. That we had a hospital that could save your leg."

He stared at her in confusion. It was obvious he didn't remember the conversation at all.

She explained the whole story to him once again. She explained how we had traveled through time to meet him. She explained that we'd brought him to Texas for medical treatment. He looked at her as if she were crazy.

"You mean I'm not in 1893 anymore?" he asked. Shock filled his face.

"No, William," I told him. "You're in the 21st century. You've traveled over 100 years into the future."

After a few seconds, his face filled with anger.

"Take me home right now!" he shouted.

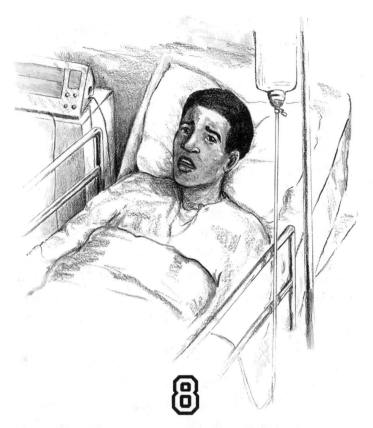

8

A Whole New World

"We can't take you home yet," Mom said gently.

"Where's Elizabeth?" William asked. He glanced around the room nervously.

"She's still back in 1893," Mom explained. "She's at home safely sleeping. She won't even realize you're gone. And when you're well, we'll take you back to her."

He lay back down on the bed. He didn't say another word. But his eyes constantly inspected the room around him.

We decided to give him a few minutes. He needed to recover from the shock.

During that time, Dad arrived. He and Mom began telling William how our time travels began. They explained how Grandpa had invented the time machine. They told him about the trips we'd already taken.

Dad described how we'd chosen to visit Cambridge. He told William about the trivia question that had led us to him. He'd also wanted to see an early football game, Dad explained.

He also reminded William of the accident. He explained that we were afraid for him. We knew he could lose his leg or even his life. We felt we had to bring him home with us. Dad explained about the hospital and modern medicine.

Mom told William how the doctors had sewed up the wound. She described antibiotics. She explained how they fight bacteria and stop infections.

William listened quietly. He never asked a question or made a comment. It was hard to tell if he believed them.

"This is a lot to hear at one time," Mom said. "But just remember that we're trying to help you. And we'll return you home safely when your leg heals."

"There's one thing we ask of you," Dad said seriously. "You can't tell anyone that you're from 1893. Only our family knows about our time travels."

"That's right," Mom agreed. "We've made up a story about who you are."

The door suddenly opened. A nurse entered the room.

"Good afternoon," she said cheerfully. "We're glad to see you're awake, Mr. Lewis."

We watched nervously as she took his temperature. William cooperated but never spoke.

"I'll let Dr. Wilson know that you're awake," she said.

As soon as she'd gone, Dad returned to William's bedside.

"I told everyone you're my nephew from Massachusetts," Dad whispered. "I said you cut your leg in an automobile accident."

Just then, the door swung open. Dr. Wilson entered the room. He walked over to talk to Mom and Dad first.

"You got him here just in time," he said softly. "Another 12 hours and we couldn't have saved him."

"But will he be okay?" Mom asked.

"I think so," he replied. "We'll keep him on antibiotics for a couple of weeks. That should finish killing any infection."

"What about his leg?" I asked anxiously.

"I believe it will be fine," Dr. Wilson said.

I was so relieved. But poor William looked scared to death. He probably thought the doctor was giving us bad news.

"I think William is worried," I hinted.

Dr. Wilson turned and saw that William looked upset.

"Hello, William," he said kindly. "Tom tells me you're his nephew."

"Yes, sir," William said softly.

"Well, you're a lucky young man," he said. "We caught that infection just in time."

William looked at him but didn't speak.

"Who stitched up your leg the first time?" Dr. Wilson asked.

"It was a young medical student," Mom stated. "He was William's friend."

"Well, I'd advise you to use a real doctor," Dr. Wilson stressed. "Your friend might make a wonderful doctor someday. But in this case, you needed better medical attention."

"We'll let you leave the hospital tomorrow," he continued. "But you'll have to rest. And take your medicine for a couple more weeks."

"Does this mean you won't have to amputate my leg?" William asked. I could see the worry in his eyes.

"Of course not!" said Dr. Wilson. "Your leg is going to be just fine."

"Can I play football again?" William asked.

"Oh, sure," Dr. Wilson assured him. "Just give that leg a couple of weeks to heal. You'll be good as new."

William looked so relieved. For the first time since he'd wakened, he smiled.

He started asking questions after the doctor left the room. Once he began, he never stopped. What kind of room was he in? Why was a tube going into his arm? Why were the lights so bright?

We tried to answer all of his questions. He was so curious about the hospital room. I couldn't wait until he went outside!

We stayed with him until late that night. We explained everything we could think of. But everything we explained only caused him to ask more questions.

Grandma brought Jenny to visit for a while. They brought fresh chocolate chip cookies for William. His face really brightened when he saw Jenny. She was relieved to see that he was better.

"There's Miss Jenny," he said brightly when she arrived. "Elizabeth would be glad to know you're taking care of me."

Jenny hopped up on the edge of his bed and started chattering. She wanted to tell him everything about her school and friends.

Dad said he'd stay with William all night. Then we could go home and rest. I asked if I could talk to William alone first.

After everyone left the room, I stood next to his bed. I didn't know exactly what to say. An apology just didn't seem like enough. Before I could even speak, William smiled at me.

"It's all right, David," he said. "The doctor says I'll be fine."

"It's not all right," I said, my voice trembling. "I shouldn't have tried to climb that tower. Then you wouldn't have gotten hurt trying to rescue me."

"You showed a lot of courage climbing that tower," he said. "Only a few Harvard men will even attempt it. And you got the flag posted. You just ran into a little trouble coming back down."

He stuck out his hand, and we shook hands. I was so relieved that he wasn't angry. I felt as if a weight was lifted from my shoulders.

I lay in bed that night and thought about William. I was determined to make his visit perfect. I could show him so many things. It would be fun introducing him to the future!

9

THE HOUSEGUEST

I felt better when I went to school the next morning. Ryan and Jeff were waiting for me in the gym. I hadn't answered any of their questions the day before. Now they wanted answers.

They wanted to know all about our trip. They also wanted to know who William was and why he was hurt.

I found myself trying to cover our time travels again. I hated keeping secrets from my friends.

I told them William was my cousin and we'd visited him in Massachusetts. I told them he'd had an accident. Then we decided to bring him to Texas to see a doctor. I hoped that would be enough to end their curiosity. It seemed to work. We didn't discuss it anymore that day.

After school, Mom took Jenny and me to the hospital. Dad was there with William. I was relieved to see them talking and laughing. I'd worried that William wouldn't adapt to the changes. But by the look on his face, he was doing fine.

"What's so funny?" I asked as I entered his room.

"We've been exploring his room," Dad chuckled. "We watched a little TV and listened to the radio. Then the telephone rang. William almost jumped out of his skin."

"Did you see my bed?" William asked excitedly. "It goes up and down when I push this red button. And a nurse comes if I push this green button."

"There are lots of things to show you," I told him. "Just wait until we get you in the van."

"What's a van?" he asked.

"It's a type of automobile," Dad explained. "It runs on gasoline."

"I read something back home about that," he said.

"Two men in Springfield named Charles and Frank Duryea are trying to invent a gasoline-powered automobile."

"Yeah, that's it," I said.

"You mean those things actually work?" he asked in surprise. "I thought that sounded like a foolish idea."

"No, not so foolish," Dad laughed.

"We'll show you what they look like," Mom said. "But first you need to get dressed. Tom will help you. The rest of us will wait out in the hall."

As we waited, we heard laughter coming from the room. After a lot of noise, Dad finally opened the door.

There stood William with his crutches. He had on a pair of Dad's jeans. They were the right length but were really baggy. He was wearing a Dallas Cowboys T-shirt. He also had on a pair of Dad's tennis shoes. It was strange seeing him in modern clothes.

He smiled brightly as he shifted the crutches. Everything we did was an adventure for him. He thought riding the elevator was fascinating.

He also loved watching people. He gawked openly at them. It was so funny to watch him.

We helped him into the van. Jenny had brought a pillow to put under his sore leg.

"You have to wear a seat belt," Jenny explained. She showed him how it worked.

"This automobile is so fancy," he said in awe.

We drove out of the parking garage. William got his first good look at his new surroundings. We allowed him to stare out the window in silence.

I noticed he was gripping the armrests. In fact, he was gripping them so tightly that his knuckles were white.

"Are you okay, William?" I asked.

"There are so many automobiles!" he exclaimed. "And they're going so fast!"

"That's the way life is nowadays," Mom laughed. "Seems like everyone is in a hurry."

He didn't relax until we turned down our street. I pointed out where Jeff and Ryan lived. When we pulled into our driveway, William gasped.

"This is your house?" he asked. "You must be very wealthy to live in a house this big!"

We laughed and assured him we were not wealthy. When we helped him into the house, he gasped again.

"I've never seen such nice things," he said in wonder. "I wish Elizabeth could be here to see this."

We didn't think he could safely climb the stairs. So we decided he should sleep on the sofa bed.

Jenny fussed over him and made sure he was comfortable.

He was fascinated with the big-screen TV. I explained how the controls worked. Soon he was clicking through the channels.

Suddenly William said he was starving. So Mom ordered two large pizzas for dinner. He was shocked when they arrived.

"You get food delivered to your door?" he asked. "And it's already cooked?"

"Yeah," Jenny said. "And pizza is my favorite food."

"I've never seen food that looked like that," William said.

"It's Italian food," I explained.

"You mean it was delivered all the way from Italy?" William asked with wide eyes.

We laughed so hard that none of us could answer him. Dad started to explain but then started laughing again. William just sat there watching us innocently. He had no idea what was so funny.

"Just try it," I encouraged him. "You'll like it."

Once he tried it, he agreed that it was really good. In fact, he almost ate a large pizza by himself.

"Tomorrow is Friday," Mom explained to William. "Tom and I have to go to work. Jenny and David will be in school. We'll have to leave you home alone."

"I'll show you some more things tonight," Dad offered. "How do you feel about being alone all day tomorrow?"

"I think I'll be fine," he said. But the look on his face said he wasn't sure.

Dad and I decided to give him a tour of the downstairs. We walked him through the kitchen. We showed him where the food was kept. Again he had a million questions. He was amazed at the refrigerator and confused by the fancy cooking machines.

We suggested he eat something simple like a sandwich. But then we had to explain what a sandwich was.

We also showed him the downstairs bathroom. He'd already learned about bathrooms at the hospital. But he still turned on the water faucets. He couldn't believe there was cold and hot water.

We got him settled on the sofa for the night. I slept downstairs too, in case he needed anything.

———◆———

We only had time for a quick breakfast the next morning. Then I was off to school.

Ryan and Jeff met me in the gym. They had thought of more questions.

"My dad says William is a football player," Ryan said. "Does he really play for Harvard?"

"Yeah," I said. "He plays center position like me."

"We want to meet him," Jeff said. "Can we come over this weekend?"

"Yeah, okay," I agreed. But I worried about whether that was such a good idea.

William was sleeping when I got home from school. I went right to work on my homework. I wanted plenty of time to spend with William later.

By the time Jenny got home, he was awake. Right away, she started telling him all about her day. We spent the evening just talking and laughing. William felt like part of the family. It would be hard to see him go.

10

A CHANGE IN LIFESTYLES

The next afternoon was exciting for William. He saw his first modern college football game on television. He couldn't believe the differences in the game.

He was amazed at the padding the players wore. He was especially interested in the helmets. He said several of his teammates had been seriously hurt. He was sure helmets would have prevented that.

He was also surprised at the number of players. His team had only 11 players. They played the whole game. They also had a much shorter rest during halftime. That made them even more tired.

Dad was explaining the modern rules when the doorbell rang. I opened the door to find Jeff and Ryan.

"Can we come in?" Ryan asked. "We came to meet William."

"Uh—yeah—I guess so," I stuttered. "Come on in."

I'd forgotten to tell William they were coming! I hadn't prepared him for their many questions. I tried to think of a quick plan. I decided I'd answer most of their questions myself.

"William, I'd like you to meet my friends," I said. "This is Ryan Wilson and Jeff Chandler."

"I'm pleased to meet you," William said politely. He shook Ryan's hand. He seemed to hesitate before shaking Jeff's hand. I thought that was kind of odd.

"How's your leg?" Ryan asked. "David told us you cut it in an accident."

"It's healing," I said quickly.

"Is it true you play football for Harvard?" Jeff asked.

"Yeah, it's true," I answered again.

"Geez, David," Jeff said. "Can't he speak for himself?"

"Yes, I can speak," William said, grinning.

They asked him a ton of questions. He answered them all perfectly. They never got a hint of his true identity.

When they left, I asked William if he liked them.

"They seem like nice guys," he said thoughtfully. "But I was a little surprised."

"Why?" I questioned him.

"Because Jeff is white," he said.

"So what?" I asked.

"It's surprising that you have a white friend," he explained. "And he lives right next door to you. He comes to your house. That just doesn't happen in my life."

"You don't have white friends?" I asked in surprise.

"Only some acquaintances," he replied. "They're not really friends. We don't live in the same neighborhood. And we don't attend the same church."

"I'm sorry it's like that," I said sadly.

"Me too," he said, sounding frustrated. "It's good to see that it will change in the future."

William seemed to settle into our lifestyle more every day. Jenny kept him busy with stories about school. Jeff and Ryan also visited a lot.

When he was stronger, William attended our junior high football games. He'd watch the games carefully. Then he'd give us tips on the way home. Jeff and Ryan were thrilled that a Harvard football player was helping us with our game.

When we were gone during the day, William stayed busy. He did some exercises that Dr. Wilson showed him.

They helped strengthen the muscles in his sore leg.

Mom rented movies for him to watch. She picked ones that showed lifestyles over the past century. She thought that was a good way for him to see our past and his future.

William watched TV too. He enjoyed the science channel most. He couldn't believe that men had gone to the moon. He was shocked that someone had actually *walked* on the moon.

He didn't like to watch the news. He was depressed by the violence and crime. It wasn't something he looked forward to in his future.

Once William's leg was stronger, we planned a surprise. We took him on a trip to Dallas. Dad got tickets to see the Dallas Cowboys play in Texas Stadium.

William was overwhelmed by the size of the stadium. After it filled with people, he became uneasy. He said he'd never seen so many people in one place.

Jenny told him the stadium would hold 65,000 people. She shouldn't have told him that. It just made him more nervous.

Mom mentioned the price of the tickets. William almost fell out of his chair. He couldn't believe they cost between $36 and $62 each.

Actually, everything about professional football surprised him. He was amazed at the playing field. He was stunned by the announcers and lit-up scoreboards. Once again, he was surprised there were so many players. While his team had 11, the Cowboys had 45. But he was very happy to see so many African American players.

William had his first hot dog during the game. He liked it so much that he ate two more.

It was fun to watch his expressions during the game. He was so excited to be there.

Afterward, we had another surprise for him. We took him to Six Flags Over Texas. We knew the 200-acre theme park would impress him. He said he couldn't have imagined such a place in his wildest dreams.

I didn't think he'd go on the rides with us. But he surprised me and joined right in. He even rode the Shock Wave double-loop roller coaster. He also went on the Roaring Rapids, a white-water boating ride. He liked it because we got soaking wet.

We both refused the Texas Chute-Out though. It was a 17-story parachute drop. We remembered our experience on the tower. Both of us agreed we'd rather stay on the ground!

It was late in the evening when we drove home. William had walked a lot that day. He said his leg was just a little sore.

But overall he seemed to be recovering quickly. He did his exercises every day. At his next check-up, he got some good news.

"The leg looks good," Dr. Wilson assured him. "You can go back to your regular activity now."

"What about football?" William asked. "Can I play football now?"

"Just give it one more week," Dr. Wilson said. "Then you should be fine to play football."

"That's good news," Dad said as we left the doctor's office.

"I'm very thankful to you and your family," William said. "But I'm ready to go home. I miss my life with Elizabeth."

"I can understand that," Dad said. "Let's just wait one more week. Then we'll take you back."

"What about the Harvard-Pennsylvania game?" William asked worriedly. "Are you sure I won't miss it?"

"You'll be there," Dad said, smiling.

William seemed satisfied with Dad's promise. I felt sorry for him though. I knew he was anxious to get home.

I was sure going to miss him. But I was relieved he'd be going home soon. After all, it was my fault he was here. And I wasn't going to relax until I knew he was safely home—home in 1893 where he belonged.

11

A Joyful Reunion

The week seemed to pass slowly for William. We did our best to keep him busy. But he spent a lot of time quietly staring out the window. He really seemed to miss his life in Cambridge now.

When the day came to return home, his whole mood changed. He was happy again.

He teased Jenny. He said he was going to keep her in 1893. He wanted her to be his little sister.

They had become close in the past weeks. It would be hard for them to say good-bye. It would be hard for all of us to say good-bye.

We packed our 1893 clothes for the weekend trip and drove to Grandma's. On the way, William got his last good look around.

"What do you think, William?" Dad asked. "Would you rather live in 1893 or the future?"

"I think I'd rather stay in 1893," William said thoughtfully.

"You would?" I asked in surprise. "Why?"

"I like quiet afternoons on the porch with Elizabeth," he said. "And the smell of smoldering hickory logs in winter. I love the smell of fresh air blowing through open windows.

"I don't have fancy things like you have," he admitted. "But I have a good life."

"As for equality between white and black folks," he said, "I'm willing to fight for that. I'm going to finish getting my law degree from Harvard. I'm even thinking about running for political office someday."

His words made me smile. I remembered what William would accomplish in his lifetime.

First he'd have a celebrated football career. Then he'd serve in the Massachusetts House of Representatives. Later he'd be appointed Assistant District Attorney of Boston.

His biggest accomplishment would be in 1910. President Taft would appoint him United States Assistant Attorney General. He'd be the first African American appointed to that position. William would spend his life breaking down barriers for African Americans.

As we rode, it suddenly dawned on me. I hadn't just spent time with a great football player. I'd also spent time with a great man. Because of men like him, my life was better.

When we arrived at Grandma's, she was waiting in the garage. She was anxious for William to inspect the time machine. He'd been so sick when he arrived. He hadn't been able to really look at it.

He shook his head in wonder. He touched every dial on the inside. Then he came back out and examined the outside.

"I don't know what to say," William said in disbelief. "This is the first time I've been at a loss for words."

We laughed and shuffled him inside. Dad set the controls to return to the same night we left. We would arrive at five minutes past midnight.

We would return William to his house. Hopefully, Elizabeth would still be sleeping. She'd be unaware he'd ever been gone. We were going to let William decide if he'd tell her about his journey.

Dad gave us the final warning. Then he pushed down on the button. William looked nervous when the ride began. I tried to focus on his face, but it was quickly lost in a blur. Moments later, the motion stopped and the lights faded. We were back in the pasture once again.

"We're here!" William exclaimed. "I can't believe it really worked!"

He was so excited. He ran ahead of us to the carriage. The horses were still tied to the fence post. We climbed into the carriage. William cracked the reins to hurry the horses along.

When we arrived, everything was quiet. William, Mom, and Jenny sneaked quietly into the house. Dad and I worked to unhitch the horses.

Once inside, we found Elizabeth sleeping peacefully. William was watching her and smiling. We talked about whether we should wake her. We decided we'd let her sleep. After all, she'd really only slept for a short time.

◆

I awoke early the next morning. I heard someone stirring in the room. It was Elizabeth. She was starting a fire in the fireplace.

I watched her as she went to William's side. She placed her hand on his forehead. Her touch caused him to open his eyes and smile.

"William!" she almost shouted. "Your fever is gone!"

"Yes, I feel fine," he said.

"Let me check your leg," she said. She pulled back the covers. I saw the surprise on her face.

"It's completely healed!" she said in shock. "How could that be?"

"Must have been your Granny's poultice." He grinned.

"But it couldn't have healed so fast," she said with a puzzled look. "It's like a miracle!"

He still had a big grin on his face.

"You know something you're not telling me, William," she whispered.

"Let's just be thankful for now that it's healed and I'm fine," William said. "I promise we'll talk about it later."

"I'm so thankful that you're well!" she said, hugging him tightly. "I don't even care why."

Elizabeth fixed a big breakfast to celebrate his recovery. William ate two stacks of flapjacks with maple syrup.

Afterwards, he announced that he was going to football practice. Coach Stewart had planned drills at Jarvis Field.

"You should rest today," Elizabeth fussed.

"I have to go to practice," he told her. "I promise I'll be careful."

She finally agreed, but she worried about him all day.

There had been so much excitement over William's injury. We'd completely forgotten that Thanksgiving was the next day. It was also William's birthday.

As soon as he left, we started preparations for Thanksgiving. Elizabeth planned a dinner and birthday celebration after the game.

William was gone for most of the day. When he returned, he said he felt strong. But we convinced him to relax that evening. We even got him to go to bed early.

The next morning, he left right after sunrise. He had to meet the team by 7:30. We finished some last minute preparations for dinner. Then we left for the big game too.

At Jarvis Field, people were coming from all directions. Some came in fancy carriages and tallyhos. Others came on horseback. Excitement filled the air.

Before the game started, a new scoreboard was unveiled. It had been invented by a man from Boston. It was the first football scoreboard ever used!

But the biggest surprise came next. Coach Stewart walked out onto the field. He asked for silence and then made his big announcement. The football team would have a new captain—William Henry Lewis!

We stood and joined in the applause. Dad whistled

loudly. William walked out onto the field and waved proudly to the crowd. Elizabeth was so excited that she cried.

The game began. Once again, we saw very few rules in the game. We saw players push and pull their teammates along. One player actually carried another one forward several yards. Several times the ball carrier crawled with the ball until he was held down.

Lots of great plays were made that day. My favorite was when the Harvard player blocked a punt. He fell on the ball behind the Pennsylvania goal. By doing that, he gained some points for Harvard.

I held my breath as a Quaker teammate charged the Harvard goal. William caught him on the four-yard line. He brought him down just short of a touchdown.

It was a hard-fought war. But Harvard was the winner in the end. The score was 26 to 4.

William came running up to us after the game.

"I can't believe I'm captain of the team!" he said happily. "What a great birthday present that is!"

"I'm so proud of you." Elizabeth smiled. "Let's go home and celebrate."

We talked excitedly all the way home. William explained some of the plays to Dad and me. And he assured us that his leg didn't hurt at all.

It was a perfect Thanksgiving Day. We had so much to be thankful for.

12

A PROMISING FUTURE

Our Thanksgiving dinner was awesome. Elizabeth
fixed wild turkey and stuffing. She made a delicious
cranberry sauce from fresh cranberries. Different
vegetables and fresh bread completed the meal. But my
favorite was the dessert. She made the best pumpkin
pies I'd ever tasted.

After dinner, Elizabeth gave William his birthday
gift. It was a warm wool sweater that she'd made

herself. His eyes shone brightly as he thanked her.

Later that evening, William, Dad, and I went for a walk.

"I'm sorry, William," I said. "We don't have a birthday present for you."

"You've given me the best birthday present ever," he said. "You gave me a glimpse of the future. No one has ever received that before."

I thought about that for a minute. It would be cool to get a glimpse of *my* future. What was the world going to be like in 2020? I wondered if the time machine could take us to the future . . .

I shook myself out of my daydream.

"Are you glad to be home again?" I asked. I was sure I already knew the answer.

"Very glad!" he said, chuckling. "And I feel a lot better too. Before the accident, I was frustrated. I was tired just thinking about the battles ahead of me."

"What do you mean?" I questioned him.

"The battles I face as a black man," he explained. "I find myself fighting for fair treatment every day. It gets very discouraging."

"I can understand that," Dad said thoughtfully.

"But now I've seen the future," William said. "It encourages me to keep going."

"We can't tell you exactly what's in your future," Dad said. "But we can tell you this. Your life will definitely make a difference. Because of your struggles, life will be easier for African Americans in the future."

"That's all I need to know." William smiled peacefully.

Our walk didn't last long. The night air was too cold. Soon we were sitting in front of the fireplace again.

"You've been a wonderful hostess," Mom told Elizabeth. "But it's time for us to return home. This is the last time we'll be able to see you."

"Oh, I wish you could stay longer," Elizabeth cried. "I've enjoyed you and your family so much. And you were such a help with William."

"I'm sorry I ever climbed that tower," I said meekly. "Then William wouldn't have been hurt."

"Don't you worry about that," Elizabeth said. "Granny says something good always comes out of something bad."

"She's right," William said and winked at me.

William's forgiveness made me feel a lot better. I was glad to know that we had given him hope too.

Saying good-bye was always hard on our trips. This time was no different. Jenny hugged William and Elizabeth several times. She just didn't want to say good-bye.

"You've been a good friend," William said as he

shook my hand.

"Thanks, William," I said. "I'm lucky that I was able to get to know you."

"Thank you, William," Dad said when they shook hands. "Thank you for all that you've done. And thank you for all that you'll do."

When we opened the door to leave, Jenny squealed loudly.

"It's snowing!" she said as she ran outside. "It's really snowing!"

I turned around and got my last glimpse of William. He was standing in the doorway with his arm around Elizabeth. I didn't need a camera because I knew I'd always remember that picture.

We walked the short distance to the pasture. The snow was beginning to pile up along the road. When no one was looking, I gathered enough for a snowball. I aimed carefully and got Dad right in the back. That started an all-out war. A constant rain of snowballs followed until we reached the pasture.

We climbed the fence and crept through the darkness. We'd just found the right place when I saw lights beginning to flash.

Lights swirled around us as we stood in that cold, dark field. We drifted effortlessly through time once again. When the motion stopped, we were safely in the time machine.

As always, Grandma was waiting. She opened the door and helped us out. We assured her we were okay. We also told her that William had been returned home safely.

We promised Grandma we'd tell her about the trip later. We just wanted to go home now.

Silence filled the van as we drove home. When we arrived, the house felt kind of empty.

I trudged upstairs to get ready for bed. I clicked on the light in my room. I was really going to miss William hanging out with me.

I went to the dresser for some clean clothes. When I pulled out a T-shirt, a piece of paper floated to the floor. I picked it up and held it under the lamp. It was a letter from William.

David,

Remember that football is only a small part of your life. Get a good education. Then you can break down barriers for those who follow you.

With warmest regards,

William

I'd never thought of my future that way. I knew there were lots of people who had worked hard to make changes. But I never thought about my chance. I had the opportunity to break down more barriers for African Americans. I could make a difference.

I wasn't sure if I'd ever play football in the pros. And I wasn't sure if I'd be accepted to Harvard. But I was sure of one thing. David Smithers was going to make William Henry Lewis proud.